Circus Freaka

Text copyright © 2017 by Hyonjun Yun and Han Kang. Interior illustrations copyright and Cover illustration copyright © by Yoojin Kang. All right reserved. Published by ACADEMYBOOK PUBLISHING, INC., 27, Dongsomun-ro13ga-gil Seongbuk-gu, Seoul, KOREA. ZIP.02832
Phone: +82–2–927–2345
Fax: +82–2–927–3199
E-mail: academybook@hanmail.net

ISBN 978-89-5681-171-0 / 03810

Printed in KOREA

이 도서의 국립중앙도서관 출판시도서목록(CIP)은
e-CIP홈페이지(http://www.nl.go.kr/ecip)와 국가자료공동목록시스템(http://www.nl.go.kr/kolisnet)에서
이용하실 수 있습니다. CIP제어번호 : CIP 2017024917

By Hyonjun Yun and Han Kang

Illustrated by Yoojin Kang

ACADEMYBOOK

Dedicated to:

The Red Fox Wheels

the best women's wheelchair basketball team in Korea

Most sincere thanks to:

Ms. Mika Wells

for the amazingly fun literature classes

and for her help in the writing process

The hardest step

she ever took

was to blindly trust

in who she was.

Harper Lee, *To Kill a Mockingbird*

PREFACE

Before you read this story, we want you to look up the Red Fox Wheels, a women's basketball team in Korea, whom this story was inspired by. Their resilience despite their, what most would consider, limited physical capabilities is beyond amazing to see. Megan in *Circus Freaka* is modeled after every member of that team who displays astounding passion, perseverance, and persistence.

While reading this story, there are many allusions and intentional literary "Easter eggs". There are references to real athletes, singers, physiologists, and more. There are some symbolism, déjà vu, and more that make analyzing the story a fun exercise. Hopefully, you can find them all as it makes the story that much more exciting.

This short story was a collaborative effort by Hyonjun Yun, Han Kang, and Yoojin Kang. Hyonjun focused on the general plot; Han wrote the rhymes; Yoojin drew the lovely illustrations. The story is structured in a way similar to a musical: there are monologues of rhythmic lines inside a traditional narrative structure.

Most importantly, we hope you enjoy the story. It was our intention to empower people, no matter their circumstances. We all live difficult lives in our own unique ways. But, as you would see Megan do, all we need is to believe in ourselves, find our strength inside us, and find that bit of luck near us.

Hyonjun Yun
Han Kang
Yoojin Kang

CHAPTER
1

A long time ago, in a place far, far away, Megan looked upon her fellow classmates riding their donkeys, horses, and mules. They were using netted sticks to toss a rough brown ball amongst each other. Each goal was worth five points, and free throws were granted one point. Once in a while, the striker would whip the ball at the opposition's colored wall, making a loud cracking noise that sparked cheers from the townspeople.

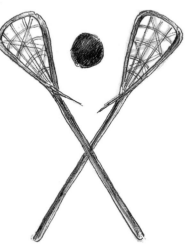

While Ghurdy, the away team, lowered their heads in disappointment, Megan's neighbors jumped from their seats, pumping their fists in the air. She, however, gave a heartless applause as she longingly looked at Jason Bolton celebrate his goal by wildly waving his arms upwards. When the final whistle blew, the entire Riverton population rushed down to the field to celebrate beating their local rivals. Megan was pushed to the ground for she could not sustain the force of a rush of 120 people with her two crutches.

Megan shakily rose from the ground, her clothes covered in footprints. The mob disbanded, and she could hear Uncle Neb calling his name from a distance. Megan stumbled to her foot to quickly stay out of the sights of her uncle. She weakly wobbled as her crutches clicked the ground in unsteady intervals. She panted hard, fixing her gaze at a nearby log that could serve as cover.

Uncle Neb shouted in an angry yet concerned tone, "Megan! I see you there. Stop, please. You will go back home with me right now!"

Megan stopped and gave a shaky sigh. She closed her eyes and continued to stumble forward till she collapsed, and the tears broke the dam in her eyes. Neb ran forward and embraced his sobbing niece.

He whispered, "It's okay, my child. Let's go home. Oh dear, oh dear," Neb groaned as he wiped her face, "What happened..."

Neb hoisted her up onto his shoulder and held her crutch in his left hand. They both slowly walked back home, leaving only snivels and tears along the way.

CHAPTER 2

Megan hopped to the armchair beside the lowly fireplace emitting a slight ember that occasionally crackled the timber. She gently swayed her right leg and left thigh to and fro. Despite what happened earlier today, she was buzzing when imagining the upcoming Ricketball World Cup that happens every four years. In all the counties of Fairhaven, Riverton was chosen as the host city which brought much joy to the locals but also a more direct pain to Megan who cannot play.

Uncle Neb strode over to the living room with a tray of biscuits and milk in hand.

He said gently, "Megan. About today, I spec-"

His niece interrupted, "I know, Uncle. You don't

need to tell me again.
I should give up
on ricketball! I
should not have
been to that game.
Blah! Blah! But I
don't care! I want to
play. I want to watch the

games. I *will* be the greatest player of all time!"

"Look at yourself Megan. It hurts me to say this,
but you can't even stand on your own two feet!"
Neb stopped suddenly, his face turning pale and eyes
widening.

Megan looked down. Her mouth shivered, and her
eyes watered.

"I'm sorry... I should not have said that. You know
what I meant. It was just a figure of speech."

"Well, it's true," Megan growled, "You meant it."

Megan's sadness turned into fury. She threw the
biscuits into the fireplace and spilled the milk over the

rug. She grabbed her crutches and stormed out the house.

CHAPTER 3

Megan did not know where to go, so she decided
to head downtown. She went inside a café by the Ayles
River. She ordered coffee and sat at a seat meant for two.
Looking out the glass walls, Megan watched the sun
simmer down into a warm sunset. She looked back at her
cup and gave a slight jump at the sudden presence of a
well-dressed man sitting across her table.

Megan squinted at the sight of the man in a well-
fitted suit with a comfortable golden chain across the
lower vest, posh bowler hat, sandy skin, and the loudest
red bow tie. The stranger had his fingers crossed and his
eyes shadowed by the domineering hat. The man leaned
back and revealed himself by exquisitely removing his

bonnet. He pushed back his silky hair to ensure that no strand was out of line.

The guest said in a thick milky tone, "Hello, Megan. I need your help."

CHAPTER
4

Megan was bewildered by her acquaintance. His dress was shockingly extravagant for a resident of Riverton. As if that were not enough, the request for help surprised Megan even more.

'I've never been asked for help... People only told me to go mess up somewhere else. Me help? What?'

She accidentally blurted her last thought out loud. The man gave a hearty laugh but quickly replaced his amusement with a trace of concern that creased his fair skin. He leaned over and opened his palms.

"I am terribly sorry for my sudden intrusion. Please forgive me. My name is Lord Pavlov. You are Megan of Poenitet, yes?" waiting for the other's confirmation, Pavlov continued, "I heard many things about you, Megan. It is an honor to finally meet you. I had to meet this hero of Riverton myself to reach out my hand. You see, ma'am, the stories I've heard... I cannot help but notice that you are being ignored! A great, young lady with great talents, yet here she is all alone. I could not bear to live knowing that I did not in some way help you with all my powers."

"What do you mean by me having great talents? You don't even know me. And I most certainly do not know you. I don't know where you got your information, but it seems like you found the wrong Megan. Now please, excuse me."

"Tut tut... This is graver than I thought. No great talents you say? Why look at yourself! Here is a young lady all alone at night with no fear in the world. These are dangerous times for Riverton, with so many tourists from all over Fairhaven, you don't know what to expect! But here you are," grinning widely to reveal a set of perfectly aligned shining teeth, "no leg yet no fear."

Megan shuffled his feet uncomfortably. She could feel her cheeks' temperature rise in an eclectic emotion of gratitude and embarrassment. Noticing the child's uneasiness, the elder rose from his seat.

He placed a calm hand on her shoulder and said gently, "Mull it over, my friend. And when you think the time is right... You'll know where to find me."

Lord Pavlov gave a subtle wink and slipped a small rectangular paper underneath Megan's hand. He strode out the café. Megan turned over the paper and was amazed to see two box office tickets for the Ricketball Finals.

CHAPTER 5

Megan excitedly hopped back to her uncle's cottage. Even from afar, she knew she was approaching the blacksmith's house. Today, the pungent smell of smelting iron was aromatic like the most delicate roses. The sharp clangs of the hammer were the voices of cupids. She firmly held onto her ticket, checking to see if it were in her hands every now and again. She briskly moved across the front lawn. It was the first time she never took a rest when coming from the town center on foot. Her heart fluttered like a hummingbird. Her cheeks hurt from smiling. She panted in the heat; it was the dog days after all.

She burst into the forge where Neb was fixing a

glowing rod on an anvil. The rod was of the most peculiar design – clearly a design unlike the blacksmith's original intent.

"Uncle! Look what I got!"

Neb placed his dark goggles above his forehead and squinted at the sudden brightness. More surprising to him was the sunnier face in his niece. He noticed her proudly holding up two small slips of paper.

"Bring me my glasses, my child. You know I can't read that," said he in a patient yet slightly excited tone.

Megan obliged and quickly retrieved his spectacles from the house.

He put them on and read, "75th Ricketball Finals. Seat A1, Royal Box. All Access Pass. Date: June 28th."

Turning the ticket over, he saw an ornate signature that was too intricate to read. The second one was the same ticket for Seat A2. Neb's breath got taken away. In his hand were two sheets of paper that was worth more than all his property and his debt. It could change his life around.

"Where did you get this, Megan? Please, tell me you didn't steal it."

"No, Uncle. A man... I think his name was Lord Palace? Palvic? Anyways, he gave it to me at the café! Can you believe it? Let's go!" Megan barked.

"Woah. Hold on, girl. Who is this man who calls himself Lord?"

"I don't know. He looked rich! He knew my name! And who cares who he is? These are genuine tickets, Uncle. No mistake about it. Gee, I can't wait to go!" Megan gushed.

"Hmm... You're right. They are real. But let's be real about this, Megs. This is enormously expensive. And why would a person you don't even know give it to you? And let's say this is really ours... we can use this to clear our debts. Imagine how much we can sell this for! I can finally get that anvil and fix that..." Neb stopped, noticing his niece's twisted face erupt in anger. She exploded,

"25 years of this career

But it's clear

Everyone sneers and jeers

Behind your back and ears

You've spiraled like Britney Spears

Back in 2007

But Pavlov, a savior from heaven

Bumping in eleven McLaren's

Beloved by everyone

A white dove among the grey pigeons

But you don't see the virtue in him

The Mets and the Yankees

Emile Heskey and Thierry Henry

Guess the ashes have blinded you

Greatest opportunity for me

And you tryna pin me down

A useless stank

That's who you be."

Megan curled herself into a ball in the corner of the dingy room. She sobbed and howled. Nothing ever seemed to go her way. Neb was taken aback. It was true. He was in massive debt. The tax collector visits every week, hounding him to pay his overdue expenses. And every week, Neb had to beg for more time, making promises, which he cannot keep, that he will pay back more than he owes. Despite his financial woes, he loved his niece more than anything.

"Don't cry, honey. Let's go. You're right. I was just caught up with myself... I can't wait to watch the Finals with you," Neb said gently with a smile, "Come on. Let's go get ready for the game."

Megan sniffled. Her red face subdued. She hugged her uncle tightly and went to her room.

CHAPTER 6

Uncle Neb, alone in his forge, sighed. He looked around, counting the things he bought with loans that were still unpaid. As the tally went above the limits of his fingers and toes, he stopped. It was unbearable to think about how he could not provide for Megan. Her parents entrusted him with her during their fatal trip to the jungle searching for diamonds.

"I was 18 years of age
First page of the high school newspaper
Up on front stage of the fame
Captain of the high school ricketball
The most popular girl, I would date her
But later

When breaking a leg
Became more than an idiom
Estranged from the pro life
No lies I blamed the guy
Who broke the bone
Below the thigh
But now I know
My own foolishness
Landed me in this pit
Now an adult
Experienced pain first
Attempting to discuss
To my dead brother's daughter
Preventing her to play
The sport that will
Slaughter her good days."

He poured water
over the furnace and
solemnly went to his
bedroom.

CHAPTER
7

It was finally the day of the Ricketball Finals. Megan waited for this day to come for a long time. In actuality, she only waited three days, but to her, it seemed like eternity.

"Come on, Uncle Neb! We're going to be late!" cried Megan from the front gate.

Uncle Neb clumsily came out of the cottage with a few water bottles and snacks. He could not contain his excitement as well.

They made their way down to the stadium. Megan wagged her parasol and whistled along with the birds. The sun beamed down on them. A few clouds could be seen in the distance but that did not worry her. Today was going to be a perfect day.

Horns and trumpets could be heard in the distance. On the sides of streets, vendors sold scarves, posters, ricketballs, and other memorabilia. Neb and Megan made it to the bright stadium. It was adorned with the colors of Riverton and Foxtown, blue and orange respectively. They went up to the Royal Box and found their seats. Neb and Megan sat down on their seats and waited excitedly for the game to begin.

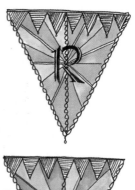

Suddenly, a group of cameras flooded in front of them and snapped away. Megan beamed. She and Neb exchanged excited looks. She was finally being recognized. In the midst of the chaos of the cameras, she heard, "Look over here, Lord Pavlov!"

Her smile faltered. The cameras were not for her.

She looked back and gasped in shock. There was a giant
tiger. It stood royally and powerfully yet its eyes were
tired. Next to it was a man who loosely held the chained
leash. The man was the impressive figure from the café.
He wore an impeccable white suit, a green bowler hat,
green designer sunglasses – despite the clouds starting
to appear overhead – and carried a rich mahogany cane.
Lord Pavlov's hair was perfectly combed back. His
entourage consisted of brawny men wearing dark black
suits. He posed for the camera, twisting his remarkably

flexible body into a series of wild yet handsome postures. After a while, he noticed the two relatives dressed in a considerably lower standard than to the rest of the people inside the Royal Box.

Lord Pavlov spread his arms and spoke with a booming voice, "Look who made it! Megan, I'm glad you came! Everybody please. Are you blind? She is here and you're taking pictures of me and not her! Give her the credit she deserves, people!"

The cameras chattered away in her direction. A minute later, Pavlov dismissed them with a wave of a hand and sat down on seat A3, next to Megan. The tiger lied down beside him with its head on its paws. He extended his hand to greet her. He reached over her to address her uncle.

"Hello, and you are Megan's...?" he asked.

"Uncle. I'm her uncle. Neb Poenitet. Thank you for the tickets, sir. You cannot understand how grateful I am for your genero..."

Pavlov interrupted, "Cool. I'm Lord Pavlov. Well

you know who I am. Ha-ha! So Megan. Tell me. How are you enjoying the game? Would you like to bet? I reckon you would bet for your town, so I'll bet on Foxtown. How about 5,000 marks?"

Megan stuttered to reply. Her eyes were fixed on the tiger. Pavlov noticed and grinned at her reverence.

"That is my tiger named Melissa. Go on and pet her," said Pavlov.

Megan hesitantly stretched her hand. Her uncle quickly grabbed her outstretched arm. She looked at Pavlov, waiting for an answer. Pavlov simply jerked his head toward the cat with a mischievous smile. She freed herself from her uncle's grip and, with her tongue out, moved closer to Melissa. The creature roared, and Megan scrambled into her uncle's arm in terror while the nobleman gave a hearty laugh. At that moment, the game began.

CHAPTER 8

The crowd cheered in support of their town. It was a beautiful spectacle. The seats were decorated with rich blue and bright orange that glimmered in the sunlight that peeked through the clouds. The professional ricketball players were riding on bizarre animals, some that Megan did not even know the name of. The goalkeepers protecting their colored walls were riding on towering giraffes; the shooters were riding on nimble ostriches; the midfielders were riding on massive creatures. Riverton's walls were in blue and Foxtown's walls were in orange. Megan could recognize that some were bulls but the others she could not recognize. Some were massive, gray beasts with horns on their snouts.

Some looked like gentle giants that had ginormous mouths, small ears, and short legs.

"Megan, do you want to be a ricketball player when you grow up?" asked Lord Pavlov curiously.

She nodded her head vehemently.

Uncle Neb interjected, "Remember little Megan. Ricketball is a dangerous sport! How can I live with myself if you get injured playing this barbaric game. You can dream, yes. But let's be realistic my child. I need you at the shop. You're the best blacksmithing child I know!"

"That's because I'm the only blacksmithing child, Uncle! I know I can be a good ricketball player. Lord Pavlov believes that! Why can't you believe that?" challenged Megan.

"That's right, my child! Don't let anybody tell you differently!" exclaimed Pavlov, ignoring Neb's glare, "You've got the arm strength, the balance... You're the complete package! It would be a sin for you not to become one!"

Megan beamed at Pavlov. She finally met a person

who understands her and believes in her. Uncle Neb, meanwhile, protectively put his arm around her and pulled her closer.

The score was twenty-eight to three with Foxtown in the lead. The fans clad in orange were growing wild while the residents of Riverton struggled to watch.

"Good thing we didn't make that bet, Megan! Foxtown seems to have this in the bag. Only seventeen minutes left!" Pavlov joked.

"Don't stop believing," sang Uncle Neb, smiling at Megan.

"You know, Megan. You can probably win that game if you enter. I have the best facilities at home. I can train you to become the greatest ricketball player of all time. If you want to, of course," remarked Pavlov casually while peering off into the distance.

Megan looked at him in surprise. Training would significantly increase her chances of becoming a professional player. Her eyes widened in excitement. The

sudden blare of trumpets halted her running imagination.
In that short span of time, Riverton made a stunning
comeback! They are now level at twenty-eight points
apiece! But Foxtown still had the ball with ten seconds
remaining. It would be the last shot of the game. Fans
all rose from their seats to get a better view. The orange
section half-raised their arms to prepare for celebration
while the blue clasped their hands together, praying for
a block or a miss. The Foxtown shooter stood on his
ostrich and hurled the ball. The ball arched over the air.
Riverton's captain Thomas Brady, on the giraffe, blocked
it! The orange fan section groaned and the blue cheered.
The game will be decided on free throws.

CHAPTER
9

Each player lined up to take their free throws. The game will now be decided on a best-out-of-five system. To complete the game's anxious atmosphere, a gray overcast appeared. A slight drizzle descended upon the field. Nobody took out their umbrellas, however. Megan did not even think about opening up her parasol to block her from the rain. Everybody clamored over one another to get a better view to witness potentially the greatest comeback ever in ricketball history. The orange striker would attempt to shoot first; Thomas Brady blocked it! Next, the blue striker smacked the ball at the orange wall and scored! Another orange striker on his ostrich stepped up only to miss! Another blue striker scored! A Foxtown midfielder got ready to shoot. He, Matthew Ryan, was the captain of the team. With an intricate move, Ryan hurled the ball, but Brady blocked it again! The next ball could now potentially conclude the game. In the tense moment, Riverton captain Brady, despite being a goalkeeper, stepped up. The pressure was on. With a simple stroke, he whipped the ball in a perfect spiral and scored! Riverton won the Ricketball Finals!

Megan waved her crutches wildly in the air and hugged her uncle. Confetti dropped, and all of Riverton were chanting for the town.

Let's go Riverton! Let's go!

Let's go Riverton! Let's go!

Let's go Riverton! Let's go!

Uncle Neb shouted, "Told you, Megs! You gotta believe!"

Lord Pavlov bended over and said with a grin, "Congratulations, Megan. Hope you mulled over my offer of going to train at my facility. I can let you meet Thomas too. He's a personal friend of mine. Believe me."

Megan cautiously said, "Really? But my uncle..."

"Look at him. He's too busy celebrating. It won't take long. Come on, let's go meet Thomas."

Pavlov took her hand and escorted her out of the Royal Box. After dancing wildly, Neb realized that her niece was gone, along with Lord Pavlov. He cursed as he saw the two, along with the tiger, exit the stadium. He quickly tried to follow them, but two beefy men in suits blocked his way. He tried to push them out of the way, but they stood still as stone.

Neb shouted, "Megs! Megan! Come back! Don't follow him!"

Megan did not look back as she silently obeyed Pavlov. Neb punched the men and shouted,

"Pavlov's dogs
Go bark at his knees
Ask to throw a Frisbee
Mindless freaks
Drooling over some bells
Trash of our nation

Probably got no education

Now let me hand you your first detention."

The men glared down at him and pushed him into his seat.

The man on the left replied angrily,

"Ayo dumb-o

We trod on your face

We are the gods of this place

Know your place

1000 Fahrenheit

Can't reach us

A different height

That's alright

Your lips are moving

But your hands are paper."

The other man joined in,

"Lord Pavlov

and his money, power, benevolence

The greatest cocktail

Respected like a folktale

Like Chris Sale

Hit you with a fastball"

Neb could not hear their words, however. His niece was now gone out of his sight.

CHAPTER 10

Lord Pavlov talked loudly over the chaotic celebration, almost as if he wanted Megan to only be able to hear him. He and Megan walked out of the Royal Box and down to the parking lot. An incredibly lavish car drove up in front of them.

Pavlov said impatiently, "Alright now. Get in."

He shoved Megan into the backseat of the car. After the door shut, she heard a mysterious tick with the door handle. She tried opening it again, but it was locked. Pavlov sat next to the driver's seat.

She asked nervously, "Umm... Mister Lord Pavlov, sir? So we're going to go see Thomas Brady, right?"

"Pfft. Why would he want to see you? Shut your

mouth, you one-legged freak. Or else, I'm gonna let Melissa eat her dinner early today," Pavlov said harshly.

As Megan trembled at the sight of the tiger right next to her, her head was suddenly covered by a dark bag.

Outside of the car, people were cheering, pouring champagne onto the streets, and doing somersaults. Inside the car, Megan cowered in her seat. She could not distinguish whether the thumping sounds were from the marching band's drums or from her heart. Once in a while, Melissa's whiskers frisked her legs which made Megan recoil and curl up even more.

Megan tried to keep calm and estimate the distance and number of turns to guess where they were going. But after the thirty-fourth turn, she lost all sense of direction. A saline tear rolled down her burning cheeks. She thought of Uncle Neb and how she betrayed him and not listen to him. Although she knew that he cannot hear him, she tried to send a mental message.

"Regret that I doubted you

But without you

I feel trapped inside a box.

The situation seems like a test

All the answers I marked

in red crosses,

Our school's test is 50 minutes.

Well will this test end?"

CHAPTER
11

The car came to a complete stop. After a click, the engine stopped roaring. Megan felt the door open, and a brute arm dragged her out. She could hear screeching, rumbling, metal clanging, whips snapping, and lots of hateful shouting. The bag on her head was yanked off. The sudden brightness blinded her temporarily. She covered her eyes and tried to peer through the thin slits between her fingers. After a while, her eyes adjusted, so she lowered her hand.

"I will turn you into a star," said Lord Pavlov in an unfamiliar oily voice.

"What? Where am I? Where's Uncle Neb?" Megan demanded answers.

"Oh forget that rusty old fool. Like uncle, like niece, eh? Cannot believe you were this easy to get. Should've listened to your old man, child. Oh well. Thanks for not, ha-ha!"

Pavlov let out a hearty and sinister laugh and bellowed,

"Welcome to Circus Freaka!
We have a variety of animals
from Asia, Australia, and Africa!
And you,
A distorted figure from Guernica,
Inside the café, a sudden eureka,
I felt.
And now you listen to me;
If you ever speak another complaint,
I'll paint you with pain;
A freak who reeks
Who's working for me,
All the profit for me
And all the people love it!"

At the final word, Megan was shoved into a cramp, metal barred cage. The door swung shut with a loud clang that rang multiple times in her ear.

CHAPTER
12

Megan quickly stood up from the bare, cold plate of steel. Her cell was one of many that made up the circumference of an immense, circle that resembled a circus stage. She had a view that looked into blazing hoops, slopes painted in confusing optical illusionary patterns, high-reaching trapezes, and a long array of whips. She shook the door with all her might till her veins rose and muscles ached. Unaware of the violent shaking, the padlock sat idly, wrapping its arm around the bars of the door and wall. She dropped down to the raw floors of her cell. Without warning, a small creature slammed itself against the wall shared by Megan's and its cell. The monkey gave a piercing screech while displaying its fangs covered in yellow tartar, scorching black gums, and radiating an acrid stench. Megan reflexively flattened herself to the opposite side of the wall, only to feel the coarse tail of an alligator in its slumber. Situating herself in equal distance between her two neighbors, she clasped her hands around her ears crushed her eyelids together.

A blaring song erupted from the speakers that were installed in the ceiling of the caged enclosure:

A day at the zoo is the best day
Monkeys and elephants and tigers
And so many more
Funny and wacky looking animals
If you feed them apples and bananas
They'll do anything for you
Magical tricks and show
All for fun! Fun for all!

Megan awoke confusedly from her curled state. The alligator also woke up, looking at her uninterestedly. It was focused more on the door and nervously backed itself away from it. Megan looked to her right and saw that the ferocious monkey was now quivering and imitating the scaly reptile. The monkey gave a frightened look to Megan, almost as if it were warning for her to do the same.

A group of men, how many Megan could not count, in dark, unwrinkled clothing entered the pavilion with a bar that glowed red at its end. One of the men pressed a switch that simultaneously unbolted all the cages' doors. Most animals came grudgingly out of their cells; Megan, however, pressed herself against the bars on the opposite side of the wall. The monkey was halfway out of its cell till looking back at Megan and motioning her to come out as well. She shook her head frighteningly. She kept her eyes on the men who stared back at her. With an evil grin, one of them brought the tip of their bar close to a cage. Then, a sudden shock ran up from the fingers that curled around the metal bars to her spine and spread throughout her body. Her hair tingly rose up, creating an afro. Letting go of the wall, she collapsed on the floor, gasping for air. Other animals that remained in the cell were equally electrocuted and quickly crawled out to the large circus. Megan followed suit. Once all were out, the doors all closed in chorus at the press of a button.

CHAPTER 13

Megan walked around, avoiding the men at all costs. The animals seemed to know where to go as they were performing tricks without any direct supervision. As she was looking around, she bumped into one of the men in dark apparel. Without warning, he grabbed her crutches and examined them. Megan, off balance, fell and looked up.

The man happily growled, "You won't be needing these anymore, freak."

With one swift stroke, he effortlessly snapped her crutches with his knee as if they were twigs. Megan wheezed in horror; they were the only physical reminder of Uncle Neb who made them for her. The man lifted her up with one arm so that she would stand on her sole leg.

"What's your name?" the man asked harshly.

"Megan," Megan squeaked in a barely audible whisper.

A sudden shock ran up her body again. The man held the glowing bar menacingly. He called over another man and asked his name.

"Pavlov," the other man grunted.

He repeatedly pointed at the other men who all introduced themselves with the same answer. At one point, he pointed at a parrot who also chirped the name of her kidnapper.

He lifted his arms in which all the men rang, "PAVLOV!" in unison.

The man stared into Megan's eyes again and asked, "So what is your name?"

Megan stayed quiet for a moment till she answered slowly, articulating each word, "My name is Megan."

With that, another electrocution blew away her confidence. She clutched her ribs where the electric stick pronged her. The world through her eyes rocked, and her ears rung. The man asked again three more times, but each time Megan gave the same answer with the addition of purposely mentioning her last name as well.

"We'll see how you answer after today's training," the man threatened, "Get up you one-legged freak. Get on that elephant."

The following hours, Megan did a variety of tricks as the men analyzed what she was capable of. She was ordered to perform handstands on elephants; hop through an obstacle course of hoops, tunnels, and balance beams; swim across a pool of water with alligators lurking nearby; hang her leg around a beam and do flips on a trapeze; balance herself on a tightrope. She was physically and mentally exhausted after performing the circus acts. Her sole reason for living now was to avoid the unbearable agony that came after failure or challenging the supervisors.

It was dawn. The animals and Megan huddled

around the center of the circle. Corn, pieces of bread, green meat (at least Megan thought it was meat), paltry peanuts, and other leftovers from the supervisors' meals were hurled at them. Lord Pavlov and Melissa looked down from their view on the catwalk above the animals' heads. He squared his shoulders and scaled the catwalk proudly like a regent. The animals quickly and quietly ate them. There was no arguing, but it was clear that they ate quickly to eat more than the next animal. At first, Megan tried to brush off the sand that smothered the food as best she could. Realizing that most of the food was gone with her stomach still growling, she gave up eating cleanly and swallowed down whatever she could grab a hold of.

"Watch this, Melissa," Pavlov said in a volume that was clearly meant to be heard by everyone.

He heaved a metal ball at the eating herd. The pack and Megan, making sure not to let go of the last bread, scrambled away. A lurid shriek filled up the quiet night. The ball landed on the monkey's tail. Megan hustled to the monkey while shoving her precious loaf of bread inside her pocket. She dug her heel to the sand and propelled her body onto the ball. It slowly rolled off the monkey's tail. As soon as it was off, the monkey clutched onto its tail and whimpered. The cells' doors opened, and the men waved their sticks to rush the animals back into their cages. Megan lifted the monkey and quickly hopped over to its cell. She gingerly placed it inside its cage and went inside her own cell.

Once inside, the lights went out with the sole

illumination coming from the lonely full moon in the clear sky. Megan took out her loaf of bread. Her stomach croaked, calling for something to enter it. However, she sadly looked at the bony monkey that still quivered while clutching its flattened tail. She tapped on their shared wall and put the bread in the monkey's miniscule hand. The monkey gave a short squeak in gratitude and munched down the bread. Megan looked up to see a nametag added to her cell. It read: *PAVLOV*. Beyond the nametag and on the catwalk, she saw Lord Pavlov descend down, assumingly on its way back to his manor. Melissa remained slightly behind him. Her vertical pupils glowed directly at Megan. Their eyes locked for roughly seven seconds till Melissa broke contact and followed her master.

CHAPTER 14

... Funny and wacky looking animals
If you feed them apples and bananas
They'll do anything for you...

Megan woke up from her uncomfortable sleep. Despite the song being from her joyful childhood, listening to it here gave her goosebumps; her hair stood up on the back of her neck. She looked up to see the nametag stare back at her. Reading her new name *PAVLOV* made her feel reduced to nothing more than a puppet and Lord Pavlov the puppeteer. She looked to her side and saw the monkey give a heartwarming gaze towards her until it realized that she noticed its stare. She felt slightly stronger as she remembered her uncle give similar looks as well.

The doors swung open in unison, and Megan made sure not to make the same mistake of staying behind. She looked up to see whether she had to do the heart-stopping trapeze again. Surprisingly, she saw Lord Pavlov and Melissa on the catwalk again. While the master, carrying a gilded electric rod and donning luminous, lavish robes that would rival King Louis XIV's clothing, looked around generally, Melissa had her eyes locked on Megan. Megan quickly looked straight ahead, fearful that she would be caught thinking about anything other than the circus, an act that does not go unpunished by the electrifying rod.

Megan did not look up at the catwalk but nevertheless could feel the piercing gaze shoot out of the tiger. She was conscious of every part of her body. She meticulously thought about her hands, her speed of movement, the tilt of her head, the swaying of her arms, and the timing of her blinking. She heard the air crack next to her ear – the crack of a whip. She spun around terrified. She feared that her suspicious movements will be punished, but luckily the supervisor just ordered her to get up on the dreaded trapeze.

Megan obeyed without a word. It was easier that way. She trained herself to keep her thoughts within the confines of her mind and maintain an expressionless face. She climbed up the ladder slowly – hauling herself with each rung by pushing on her leg and pulling with her arms. She climbed four separate ladders, each divided by a small platform. After climbing the last ladder, she was at the catwalk; Lord Pavlov paid no attention, but Melissa did not cease her scrutiny. Megan tried to act like she did not notice the tiger and wiped the sweat off her palms. She patted her hands with white powder and gave a series of mini hops to drive away the fear. Down below, the overbearing, menacing supervisor seemed like a harmless ant. Yet, the glowing rod in his hand was enough to convince Megan that she should not develop the courage to rebel at the moment. She took a deep breath before trusting herself on the rung suspended in the air by only two thin ropes. Her strong arms did not give way to her fear of heights, and she landed successfully on the other side of the circus. Seemingly satisfied, the supervisor stopped looking up and averted his attention to a giraffe. During her swing, Lord Pavlov went down to the ground alone to closely survey the training animals. Melissa was cautiously crawling her way towards Megan. In fear, Megan fought the urge to take a rest and swung herself across the air again. The tiger gave a low grunt in disapproval and hastened her approach to Megan who was now on the other side of the circus. Megan clasped her hands on her knee, panting for air. She was unaware of the tiger stalking behind her.

CHAPTER 15

A paw covered Megan's mouth. The fur muffled her yelp.

"Shush child," murmured the speaker behind Megan in a peculiar accent.

Megan's eyes grew wide in bewilderment. She was sure that it was the tiger, but to whom does the voice belong to?

As if the speaker could hear her thoughts, it replied, "I call myself Melissa. Yes, talk I can."

The paw relaxed, and Melissa slowly spun around to face the tiger. Melissa continued to talk, but no words entered Megan's brain. She was too enraptured by the way the cat's jowls and lips moved naturally like a human's. Noticing her lack of focus, Melissa gave a low growl. Megan shook her head and the buzz that diluted her vision went away.

"Brave, you was.

Save that monkey, you did.

Hate toward Pavlov, I see.

Same hate, I have.

Became a slave, I did.

Fooled by a bait, I did.

Attacked by a bear, he did.

Went for the aid, I did

Save, I did.

Like a fire brigade,

Tricked and betrayed.

Displayed as a slave, I did.

As he bathed in his riches.

As my courage decayed.

As my body ached.

Stayed patient, I did.

All these days wait, I did.

For a brave one,

who's awake.

To break the chains.

To set him ablaze.

To chase him away.

To escape Pavlov's cave.

For you to pave the way.

So tonight be awake."

Without given time to reply, Megan only watched as Melissa skulked back down to Lord Pavlov. On her way, she dropped a claw and grunted "take." It was the first time someone has called Megan by her actual name since she arrived at the compound. She picked up the claw and placed it inside her pocket. She could see supervisors climb up the ladder, so she hastily resumed her trapeze sequence. Her fear of heights now vanished. Every breath, every thought, and every movement was made with veiled jubilation. The thought that she was not alone in this atrocious circus brought a deluge of ecstasy. She carried out her day with relative ease. The shocks, the pain, and the insults felt muted. Megan could only wish for the Sun to fall and the Moon and stars to take its place.

CHAPTER 16

The sky turned a beautiful shade of purple with a
few speckles of clouds that
dotted the heavens.
High above the sky
sat the dim moon
that grew brighter
with each passing
minute. George
and Megan locked
eyes multiple times throughout
the day. Megan was not sure if it were by coincidence or if
George knew what would happen tonight.

After eating and covertly collecting the morsels of

food thrown at the animals, Megan went inside her cell. She made sure the claw was firmly inside her pocket. Brushing past her as he went, George silently went inside and immediately curled up into a ball and held its tail like a doll. The floodlights went out as usual, and only the moonlight filled the complex. She lied down, but her eyes did not close. A fluttering sensation packed her body. At every noise, she twisted her neck to check if it were Melissa. Judging by the displacement of the moon from when she entered her cell, hours passed. Yet, still no Melissa. George's soft, succinct breaths confused Megan. She was unsure whether any animal was awake like her or not.

Megan was focused on George's closed eyes; she reckoned that if she focused hard enough she can see through the thin eyelids and discern if he was actually sleeping or pretending to be asleep. She heard a soft thud within the training grounds of the circus. Megan was certain that somebody entered. Nervously, she canted her head in the direction of the door. Nobody was there.

A familiar voice out of nowhere hissed, "Slow, you are. Wait forever, I have. Turtle or human, I wonder. Lose claw, have you?"

"Oh I was waiting for you! Okay hold. Yeah, I still got the claw," said Megan excitedly.

"Hssss. Loud, you are. Elephant, are you?"

Megan silently chuckled and fumbled around for the claw. The tip was thin enough to go into the padlock. She twisted it around a few times until she heard a click. None of the animals noticed. She swung the door smoothly and hopped out into the circus training facility. She looked around wonderingly, searching for her feline friend. An orange deposition appeared inches from her nose as the tiger appeared seemingly out of nowhere. Aware of the situation, Megan bit her tongue to not exclaim in surprise.

Melissa murmured, "Get on, you must. Little time, we have."

"On? On what?"

"Me. Great strength, your arms. But speed, we

tonight need. Hurry."

The tiger crouched to allow Megan to saddle on her back. Melissa was soft and warm. Despite only having one leg, Megan had no trouble balancing herself on the feline thanks to her silky movement. They slid their way up the trapeze ladder rungs and onto the catwalk.

There, Megan found a pile of screwdrivers, hammers, pliers, wrenches, and drills. She slid off Melissa's back to pick it up. She finally understood  her role in their escape: she could use her ingenuity, thumbs, and blacksmith background to get out of the metal enclosure.

Melissa guided her to the end of the catwalk. Hidden in the ceiling of the dome of the circus was a bolted door – the gateway to freedom.

CHAPTER 17

Megan did not go to work immediately. She frowned in disapproval and looked at Melissa with confusion.

"Wait, how did you get inside here? Can't we just go out the way you came in?" Megan inquired.

"That door, too risky. Only connected to Master's house. Goes to, this way, outside. Fits us," Melissa said.

Melissa understood and picked up the tools to unlock the door. While she was working, she did not think about Riverton and Uncle Neb; she thought of George and the rest of the animals. They would remain trapped here and possibly have to endure retribution for not detecting their escape. Megan was about to unhinge the last bolt which secured the door before pausing. She turned around and shook her head.

"I'm not leaving without the rest," she said adamantly.

"What? Leave we must immediately. Sun rises soon. Everybody, we cannot take," Melissa said fretfully.

Megan explained,

"We talk to the mirror

'I won't become the monster I fear.'

but I doubt neither

Me or you

imagine ourselves becoming the monster we hate."

Megan began to screw the bolts back in place. Melissa placed her paw on the bolt and looked serenely at Megan.

"Very well. Out my way, we go. Through Master's house. With everybody. Come, no time to fix door." Megan hopped back on Melissa's back and descended down the ladder to return to the cells.

CHAPTER 18

Megan and Melissa quickly went to work. *Click.*
Click. One by one, the doors unlocked with a twist of a
claw, and the imprisoned animals were wakening. The
sky that glazed the horizon showed shades of warm hue.
It was a race against time – a race that Megan and Melissa
were losing. Those still inside their cells were growing
restless, banging on their cages and stretching their
limbs out of the cell. The salty precipitation on Megan's
forehead rolled down her cheeks as she tried to unlock
the door of a hairy orangutan whose luscious hair was
styled into a convoluted braid. She was trying to shush
the animals and implored them to be patient to not wake
up the supervisors. She stopped abruptly. She realized

the animals' limbs were all pointing in one direction. She looked at what the orangutan was pointing at, and it was clearly one thing that was the target of its harmonious fingering. She yelped in a moment of eureka.

"Thanks, umm... what's your name?" Megan asked excitedly.

The primate gloomily pointed at the nametag that said *PAVLOV* in harsh letters.

"No thanks. I think I'll call you Harry. Thanks, hairy Harry!" exclaimed Megan as she rushed toward the direction of its finger.

It was a small
metal box with
electrical
conduits
spreading
out of its
frame. She
opened it
and there

was a switch that was labeled CAGE DOOR. She flipped it. At once, all the doors swung open. The circus enclosure erupted in animal noises. Melissa mightily roared above the chaos to silence the animals. A light inside the manor turned on and the supervisors' voices could be heard in the distance.

CHAPTER 19

The herd of animals all fell silent; an eerie tension constituted the air. Megan climbed onto Melissa, and, together, they led the pack to a jumble of boxes. Melissa swiped away the boxes which exposed an expansive trap door that revealed a large underground tunnel. Harry the orangutan pulled the door open. All the animals followed Megan and Melissa down the tunnel.

The underpass was dimly lit. It was roughly made as if a gigantic groundhog dug it. The rocky floor was jagged and uneven. There were occasional puddles that formed from the water that dripped down from the topsoil.

The herd quietly rumbled on. A pale figure stood in the distance. It was not moving towards them but rather standing still. Despite being unable to distinguish the individual, Megan knew that the upright, imposing person was Lord Pavlov. He was twirling a cane that glowed red at the tip.

Melissa halted. The large group of animals lightly bumped into each other at the sudden stop. The animals in the back squealed, wondering what caused them to stop. The tunnel was silent except for the lowly hum from

the electric stick.

Pavlov said in a chilling tone that echoed in the confined channel,

"Come now before I make you into medicine
No human medicine?
Well it will be a new edition
A sensation
So quit this madness
Or turn this circus into a mall
Alligator Leather boots, Tiger fur carpets, Monkey stuffed doll
Plenty of meat to open a butcher
I'm the boss of this place
And you're a big disgrace."

Melissa lowered her head. She could hear the supervisors coming from their back. They were trapped in the narrow passageway. Then, the elephant trumpeted a piercing pitch, and on cue, all the animals ran in Pavlov's direction. Melissa followed as Megan clung onto her back. Surprised by the animals' confidence,

Pavlov fearfully dropped his stick and ran back towards his manor. He could not, however, outrun the animals. Megan saw him being knocked over by her neighbor alligator. Melissa ran in such speed that Megan could not find out Pavlov's fate. She never looked back to see what happened to him. In fact, she would never look back at all on her way back home.

CHAPTER 20

After exiting the tunnel, leaving out of Pavlov's –
now ruined – manor, the animals were on the open road.
The parrot flew from above to squawk the directions
back to Riverton. On the way, villagers gawked in awe at
the sight of a jumble of eclectic animals – and a human
on a tiger – walk in an orderly procession.

It took a few hours
till Megan saw a wooden
sign which told her
that Riverton was
one mile away.
She exclaimed and
punched the air

in joy. Melissa began to jog so that her friend can arrive home quicker. From afar, Megan could see the lights in her school's field which indicated that a ricketball game was in play under the scenic stars and Moon.

"Melissa, take me there," Megan said softly.

The tiger listened, and the pack went to the school. Megan could hear the shouts of her classmates. It appeared to be a game between Riverton High School and Ghurdy High School. The scoreboard read 24-25 with Riverton trailing by one point with one minute left to go.

Megan urged Melissa to go faster as they entered the stadium. The crowd all confusedly rose from their seats at the sight of a pack of diverse animals enter the field.

Megan went up to the Riverton coach, "Coach. Put me in."

The coach goggled at the tiger and did not reply. Melissa roared, the alligator snapped, the elephant stomped, George shrieked – the herd erupted.

The coach stammered, "Bol... Bolton! Jason Bolton!

Get off the field. Megan is going on."

Jason protested, "Are you kidding me, coach? Megan is a girl! She can't play ricketball. This is a man's sport!"

"Precisely why you can't play, little boy. Get off. She returned after God knows how long. And you seriously want to say that in front of... this?"

Jason looked at the snarling tiger and thought it would be better to obey his coach. He and his donkey trudged off the field.

Uncle Neb squinted to see who the substitute was. He attended every ricketball game after Megan was kidnapped in memory of her. His eyes widened when he saw that the tiger rider only had one leg. He clutched onto the person sitting next to him in order to not faint.

"Megan! Megan!" he shouted.

Megan could not hear. She was determined to win for Riverton and prove everybody wrong. She looked at the clock. The timeout ended. The minute countdown to the final whistle began.

CHAPTER
21

Megan caught the ball with her netted stick.
Megan's and Melissa's minds and bodies acted as one. No
communication was required. They were telepathically
connected. Melissa danced around the defenders.
Ghurdy's players and their group of mules and horses
could not keep up with the nimble cat. Megan looked
up at the clock again. It read 0:07 – seven seconds left.
Melissa snaked in front of everybody to leave only the
Ghurdy's goalkeeper in between Megan and the goal.
Megan snapped the netted stick with her powerful arms
to let the ball rocket towards goal. The ball eluded the
goalkeeper's fingers and smacked the brown wall. The
crowd burst in cheers as the goalkeeper's head dropped.

The animals from the circus jumped up and down, celebrating Megan's goal. The whistle blew and the game was over. Riverton won twenty-nine to twenty-five.

CHAPTER
22

Hooray for Megan! You have saved the day!
You can be captain! We don't need you, Jay!

The team swarmed around Megan, thanking her for the victorious goal. People begged her to join the Riverton ricketball team. The crowd parted to create a line. At the end of the line was Uncle Neb, hobbling over to greet his niece. Megan and Neb embraced as their sobs flooded the ground. Everybody clapped, including the players from Ghurdy.

"Hey! Woah! Umm... Excuse me! Woohoo, yay, we won. That's great. But she's a girl. She can't play for us. Who says? I says. I'm the captain," Jason said sharply.

The crowd slowly faced Jason. Their expressions were of disgust and anger. Neb tried to hide his smile. The Riverton ricketball team coach approached Jason.

"Not anymore," the coach said.

He ripped off the captain's badge. That triggered a cheer from the crowd. The coach walked over to Megan.

"Do you want to be the captain, Megan?" the coach asked politely.

Megan looked at the badge that was a sapphire R, for Riverton. She looked at Uncle Neb who nodded his head enthusiastically.

She smiled and said, "No thanks. I think I'm going to help out Uncle and become a blacksmith."

"Well, whenever you want. You're welcome to join the team any time," the coach replied.

CHAPTER 23

Four years passed since the day of Megan's return to Riverton. She was on Melissa who sped past the other players in a blur. The captain's badge glistened under the shiny day. On the leather saddle made by her uncle, Megan shifted her body comfortably to stretch and catch the ball with her netted stick. She was securely fastened to the saddle with her foot clipped to one side and a prosthetic leg, her own creation after the careful guidance and apprenticeship of her blacksmith uncle, clipped to the other. At the signal of the screeching whistle, the exhausted players and animals slowed down and gathered around the coach.

The coach confidently spoke, "Alright team. Great

practice session today. If we play like what we did today, I don't care who we face, I know we're going to win. Let's go. Team on three. One, two, three,"

"Team!" everybody shouted and went home.

Megan walked around the forgery – without her crutches – to get the hammer. Soft steps interchanged with the taps of her aluminum leg. The forgery was no longer dingy. The sunlight shone through the clear windows and cloaked the room with warmth and vivacity. Her uncle gently pulled out a glowing hot orb from the sweltering furnace and tightened it on the anvil by rotating the screws to clamp it in place. They both took turns hammering the orb to flatten it into a plate. Outside their home, a sign reading *N&M's ARTISTRY*, written in bright blue letters, hung at the front yard. Business was booming. The absurd creations made before by Uncle Neb were rebranded as art pieces. The mayor commissioned Neb and Megan to decorate the government buildings with their metal sculptures to signify the town's innovation, progressiveness, and pioneering of industrial and social issues.

Uncle Neb glanced at his watch for the tenth time in one minute. He was nervous, unlike his niece who was confidently pounding the orb without any notice of the sweat dripping down her face. It was time to leave. He nudged her and wrapped his arm around her shoulder. Megan, dressed in blue, carried her parasol, and Neb grabbed the picnic box of snacks and water bottles from the kitchen counter. As they left the house and walked down the road, the symphony of birds, trumpets, and horns filled the air. Vendors sold scarves, posters, ricketballs, and other memorabilia on street curbs. Megan and Neb entered the brightly lit stadium in separate entrances. While Neb was taking his seat, Megan lined up in a dark tunnel with a host of other players, dressed in blue and red, along with animals. She took her place next to Melissa who stood proudly at the front of the line. In front of them, at the end of the tunnel, light started to pan up from the bottom. The gates croaked up and the deafening cheers of the anxious crowd resonated the enclosed hallway. Megan hopped on Melissa. Four years ago, she reversed her decision to walk away from ricketball. She decided to play and help her uncle as well. Now, it would be the last game of her illustrious career.

"Let the 76th Ricketball Finals begin!" an announcer boomed.

Megan breathed in deeply and closed her eyes. She felt the smooth fur graze her leg. As she opened her eyes, she patted Melissa. They slowly walked forward into the blinding lights to play one more game.

THE END.